YOU ARE LOVED,

CALI ROSE

Personalized Coloring Book
by Suzanne Marshall

Note: Not Intended for Markers
Please Use Crayons or Colored Pencils

LiveWellMedia.com

ISBN: 9798364738417

This coloring book is dedicated to

CALI ROSE

who is loved, lovable and loving.

INSTRUCTIONS

* Use crayons or colored pencils (not markers).

* Color inside, outside, over, under, through the lines...

* Use any colors you wish, anywhere in this book.

* Make up your own rules, because this is YOUR book!

CALI ROSE

A bunny sitting in the sun
says you're creative, bright and fun.

CALI ROSE

A puppy dog says with a bark
that you have such a loving heart.

CALI ROSE

A musical mouse says with a squeak
that you are hopeful and upbeat,
and always get back on your feet.

CALI ROSE

A kitty cat says with a mew
that you are loved for being you.

CALI ROSE

The bees are buzzing with the news about your positive attitude.

HONEY

CALI ROSE

Butterflies flutter near and far
saying you are beautiful as you are.

CALI ROSE

In the rain quack-quacks a duck,
who says that you've got lots of pluck.
If you fall, you rise back up!

CALI ROSE

A loving pair of dancing geese
say you are full of joy and peace.

CALI ROSE

A friendly frog with polka dots
says you've got lots of happy thoughts.

CALI ROSE

A pig says (with an oink or two)
that loving you is easy to do.

CALI ROSE

A groundhog leaves his burrow to say:
you make the most of every day.

CALI ROSE

A cute raccoon, awake at dusk,
says you are loved so very much.

CALI ROSE

A little lamb says with a grin:
you try new things, and try again.
That's how you let adventures in!

CALI ROSE

A spunky squirrel with a nut
says you are loved no matter what.

CALI ROSE

A pony gallops by to say:
you listen, learn and love each day.

CALI ROSE

A baby cow (also known as a "calf")
says nothing's sweeter...
than the sound of your laugh!

CALI ROSE

A newborn chick pops out to say:
making mistakes is A-Okay.
That's the way you grow and play!

CALI ROSE

> A birdie sings from high above
> that you are truly, deeply loved.

CALI ROSE

A penguin standing in the snow
says you are smarter than you know.

CALI ROSE

A parrot sitting on a shelf
says you believe in yourself.

CALI ROSE

A giant whale says with a wink
that you are braver than you think.

CALI ROSE

A pair of fish swim by to say
that you are loved every day.

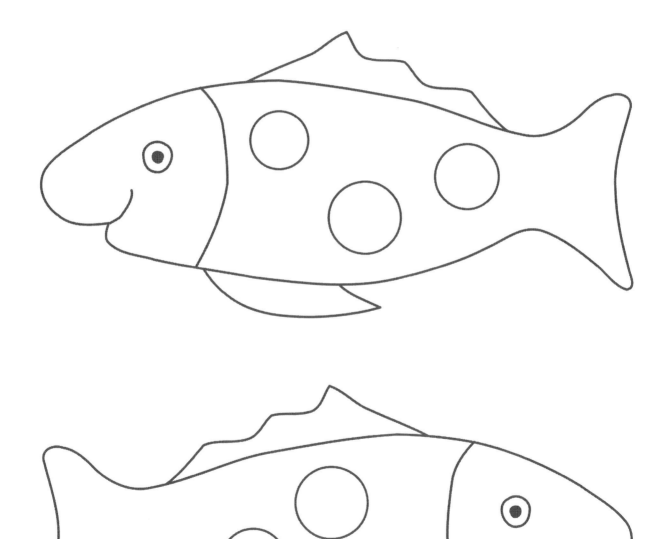

CALI ROSE

A lion wearing a little bow
says you are stronger than you know.

CALI ROSE

A kangaroo with a baby in her pouch
says you are loved...
even when you're a grouch!

CALI ROSE

A monkey chuckles with delight:
that even when things don't go right,
you see the sunny side of life.

CALI ROSE

A mighty ape says with a shout
that you are loved inside and out.

CALI ROSE

An otter playing with a bunch of balls
says you give everything your all.

Cali Rose

A koala in a eucalyptus tree
says you are loved unconditionally.

CALI ROSE

A camel says what's on her mind:
that you are friendly, helpful and kind.

CALI ROSE

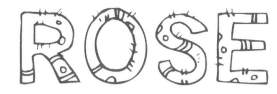

An elephant who's very clever
says you are loved now and forever.

ABOUT THE AUTHOR

Suzanne Marshall writes books to inspire, engage, and empower children. Her books are full of positive affirmations and words of encourgement.

A healthy mind is a happy mind!

An honors graduate of Smith College, Suzanne has been a prize-winning videographer, produced playwright, and teacher. Critics have called her writing "intelligent" and "very powerful." One even remarked that her story was like "a really good rhubarb pie – a certain tangy bite built into a very sweet crust." This last review made Suzanne a bit hungry! Learn more about Suzanne and her children's books at **LiveWellMedia.com**.

Made in the USA
Monee, IL
22 November 2022

18308709R00022